The Best Christmas Ever

By Dandi Daley Knorr

Illustrated by Gwen Connelly

STANDARD PUBLISHING
Cincinnati, Ohio   3545

Edited by Theresa Hayes

Library of Congress Cataloging-in-Publication Data

Knorr, Dandi Daley.
The best Christmas ever.

(A Jenny and Josh book; 3)
Summary: Trudy's troublemaking threatens to make her miss the school Christmas party until Jenny takes the blame, missing the party herself, and makes Trudy's holiday "the best Christmas ever."
[1. Christmas—Fiction. 2. Conduct of life—Fiction] I. Title. II. Series: Knorr, Dandi Daley. Jenny and Josh book; 3.
PZ7.K754Be   1987   [E]   87-6441
ISBN 0-87403-315-2

*To my niece Kelly.
Thanks for all of your
valuable assistance.*

"Five whole days before Christmas, but only one day till
our party!" shouted Jenny to Trudy as they ran down the
school steps. "And look! It's starting to snow!"

Jenny gave her doll Mindy a squeeze. "Mindy and I can't
wait! I love Christmas! Aren't you excited about tomorrow, Trudy?"

"Why should I be?" asked Trudy. "You heard what Miss Tuffy said." Trudy tried to imitate their teacher's shrill voice, "If you misbehave one more time, Young Lady, there'll be no Christmas party for you! I'll send you home with a note for your mother!"

"Then don't misbehave anymore," returned Jenny. Why did you push Tasha at recess, anyway?"

"Because I felt like it," blurted Trudy, and she ran away.

Jenny heard Katy call her from behind, "Jenny! Wait for me!" Jenny waited for Katy to catch up and then smiled as Katy asked, "Can I hold Mindy?" Jenny gently handed Baby Mindy to her friend.

"She's the best baby ever," said Katy." I hope my mom gives me a baby just like Mindy for Christmas.

As the girls neared Jenny's house, Katy sighed, "You're so lucky." She handed the baby back to Jenny saying, "Time to go to your mommy. Be good so Santa Claus will bring you something wonderful!"

Both girls giggled. "Good-bye Katy. See you tomorrow at the party," Jenny called as she ran up to her house.

Later, sitting at the dinner table with Mom and Dad and her big brother, Josh, Jenny couldn't stop talking about the Christmas party.

"Miss Tuffy says we will have to have a little bit of school first, but all the rest of the day will be our party! I drew Trudy's name for the gift exchange—yuk! I wish I'd gotten Katy's name instead!"

"Jenny," said Mother, "don't talk like that. You don't want Trudy to feel badly. She is having enough trouble, Honey. I'm sure she could use a friend."

Jenny defended herself, "But Trudy always gets us into trouble! Yesterday she threw all the potted plants right out the window—all the plants that we grew for science class!"

Josh chimed in, "And before that, she wrote her name on the wall in the front hallway! And before that—"

"OK." Father stopped them. "That's enough."

"That's exactly what Miss Tuffy said," piped up Jenny. "'That's enough, Trudy.'" Jenny shook her finger at Baby Mindy, who was sitting in her own tiny high chair next to Jenny. "'And if you do one more bad thing, Young Lady, you can't come to our Christmas party!'"

"That would be a shame," said Mother, getting up from the table with dishes in her hand. "Because your school party is probably the only Christmas celebration Trudy will have."

"Why?" Jenny asked in unbelief.

"Because the Warners barely have enough money to feed their children," explained Dad. "They can't afford presents."

"Even at Christmas?" Josh was as shocked as Jenny.

"Even at Christmas," replied Mother; "so I hope you have a very nice gift for Trudy. It may be the only Christmas present she receives this year."

Jenny was deep in thought as she got up and slowly left the room. She was thinking so hard that she forgot to take her brownie.

"Can I have Jenny's dessert?" Josh asked.

"*May* I," corrected Dad. "And yes, I guess you may."

Jenny went to her room, thinking about her gift for Trudy. When she and Katy had talked about what to give Trudy, they had decided that one of Jenny's old books—one that didn't look too worn out—would be a good enough present for Trudy.

"We better do some hard thinking, Mindy. If you were Trudy, and could get only one Christmas present, what would you want?"

As Jenny tucked Baby Mindy into bed, she got down on her knees beside the baby's crib and prayed, "Dear God, we know You gave us Your own little Son for Christmas. Please help us figure out what to give Trudy. Amen."

She got herself ready for bed and crawled in, thinking about things she could get for Trudy. Jenny thought hard, for a long time. She rejected one idea after another until at last, she fell asleep.

The next morning, Jenny walked into the kitchen dressed in her new red velvet dress. Her mother and dad greeted her with "ooh's" and "ah's."

"I'll get the camera," said Daddy, heading for the den.

"No, I'm in kind of a hurry to get to school," said Jenny, "but thanks anyway! I'm hoping that if I get there early, Miss Tuffy will let me help decorate for the party."

Jenny gobbled down her breakfast and then disappeared to her bedroom. She returned carrying a large brown grocery bag with a red ribbon tied around the top.

"Jenny," asked Mother, "is that your present for Trudy? Don't you want me to help you wrap it and make it look pretty?"

Mother reached for the bag, but Jenny was out the door and racing down the sidewalk. "No, thanks, Mom! I gotta go. Bye!"

"But Jenny," Mother shouted, "You forgot Mindy! Jenny!" But Jenny must have been too far away to hear her.

"She will be awfully disappointed when she finds that she forgot to bring Mindy to the party," Mother said to Daddy. "This is the first time since we gave her that doll that Jenny has forgotten to take Mindy with her."

Jenny arrived twenty minutes before the first bell rang. She climbed the stairs to her classroom and placed her bag on the table she was sure Miss Tuffy would use for gifts. And, Jenny was right—because she was the first student there, she was appointed party hostess. Miss Tuffy

announced that Jenny could pick one friend to help her decorate while the others went downstairs to music class.

The room filled with gasps when Jenny chose Trudy. Even Miss Tuffy had to catch her breath and ask Jenny if she had really said Trudy.

When the time came for music class, Miss Tuffy told Jenny (and Trudy) how to decorate the classroom for the Christmas party. "Jenny, you set all the gifts out on our gift table, and Trudy, you may set out the cups and napkins for our treats." Then Miss Tuffy led the other children down the hall to music class.

"This is great, isn't it, Trudy?" Jenny asked excitedly.

"Sure," said Trudy, "only you always get all the good jobs. Let's trade. I'll put out the presents, and you can get the cups and napkins."

"Well," hesitated Jenny, "I guess that would be OK." And she went to find the Christmas napkins.

Quick as a flash, Trudy scurried to the gift table and began taking off all the name tags. Then she mixed them up and placed each tag on a different present. Jenny was busy putting a napkin on each desk, and did not see what Trudy was doing.

"There!" Jenny said as she finished with the napkins, "Now I'm ready for the cups. How are you doing with the gifts, Trudy?"

"Oh, just fine," snickered Trudy, "just fine."

The children were buzzing with excitement as they filed back from music class. Miss Tuffy was humming her own version of "Deck the Halls," "Fa-la-la-la-la, la-la-la-la. All right, ladies and gentlemen," she announced, "it's time for our Christmas party!"

Just then, Katy passed the gift table. "Hey!" she yelled, "That's not the present I brought for Jeremy! *That* one is— but the tag on it says it's to Abby from Matthew!"

"I didn't bring that present," answered Matthew. "I brought *that* one." Everyone shouted as they gathered around the gift table. Miss Tuffy *really* had to yell to make herself heard.

"Sit down, everyone! To your seats this minute!" Her face turned red and she clenched her fists. "I'll get to the bottom of this!"

"Jenny! Trudy! What's going on here? Someone has switched all of these name tags! Trudy, I told you, one more trick from you and I'd send you home."

"But Miss Tuffy," Trudy said, "I just had to set out the cups and napkins. *Jenny* was in charge of the gift table."

All eyes turned to Jenny. She didn't say a word.

"Well, Jenny," Miss Tuffy said in her most shrill voice, "what do you have to say for yourself?"

Jenny bit her bottom lip. She looked at the ground. Then she looked at Trudy. They stared at each other. Finally, Jenny said, "I'm sorry, Ma'am. I have nothing to say for myself."

"Well, I never! screeched Miss Tuffy, "Then *you* will be the one to go home and miss the party!"

As Jenny left the school building, she could hear the laughter of the other children as they opened their gifts. Suddenly, all the chattering stopped. Jenny strained to hear what was happening.

The first voice she heard was Katy's. "Oh! It's Baby Mindy!" Then she heard a strange, shaky voice from Trudy.

"Jenny gave me Baby Mindy?"

Jenny left for home. As she walked, she thought about all that had happened, and how Trudy's voice had sounded. Jenny smiled to herself, and as she neared her house, she started singing,
  "A-way in a man-ger,
  No crib for a bed,
  The little Lord Jesus
  Laid down His sweet head."

Jenny was still singing when she walked into the kitchen. "My, you're in a good mood!" Mother said. "Is your party over already?"

"No, I didn't get to stay for the party," Jenny answered. "Trudy mixed up all the presents and told Miss Tuffy that I did it, so she sent me home."

"But Jenny, why didn't you tell her the truth?"

Jenny shrugged. "I figured I could take the punishment better than Trudy—that was her only chance for a party. Anyway, I wanted to make sure that she got my present."

"Oh? What did you give Trudy?" asked Mother.

"Baby Mindy."

"Oh, Jenny!" Mother knelt down and wrapped her arms around her. "You're quite a girl! And I'm *very* proud of you! Mother wiped the corner of her eyes. "And you had to miss the party! Well! How would you like to help me with these Gingerbread people, then?"

Jenny had one of Mother's aprons tied around her neck and was busily rolling out the gingerbread dough when she heard a knock on the kitchen door.

She opened it and there stood Trudy, holding Baby Mindy in her arms. Trudy had tears in her eyes and her cheeks were very red.

"Jenny," she said, "I'm sorry. I told Miss Tuffy that I was the one who switched the name tags. She was very mad, but she said you had taken the punishment for me and there was no way for me to pay you back." Trudy stubbed the doorway with her scuffed shoe. "All I can do is thank you." She looked up at Jenny. "Thank you, Jenny. I won't ever do another mean trick at school again!"

Trudy paused and looked down at her prize. "But, Jenny, you didn't have to give me your own baby doll."

Jenny smiled. "I know I didn't *have to,* Trudy. I *wanted* to give you Baby Mindy." Trudy looked at Jenny in amazement and then broke into a big smile.

"Oh Jenny, this is the best Christmas I've ever had! How can I ever thank you?"

Jenny reached out to hug Trudy, who quickly hugged her in return.

"Well," said Jenny, "you can come in and we'll play with Mindy together, because I think you're right; this *is* the best Christmas ever!"